Once There Was and Twice There Wasn't

AUTHOR'S NOTE: Many American children know the tales of Nasreddin Hoca, the beloved Turkish teacher-preacher-judge, whose antics, wisdom, and nonsense have tickled their funnybones, but few have met Keloğlan (Kell'-oh-lahn), the folk character second only to the Hoca in the appeal to Turkish listeners.

Keloğlan (bald boy) is a kind of Jack, Cinderlad, Ali Baba, and Brave Little Tailor all rolled into one. Usually the youngest of three brothers, and rejected for his apparent stupidity, Keloğlan manages to blunder through one experience after another and to win over all other contenders at the end. Lucky, almost beyond belief, he is generally good-natured and openhanded, but shrewd and not above the playing of tricks to destroy the giant or win the princess. He is the young peasant who becomes the padishah (king); he is the guesser of riddles, solver of dilemmas, and righter of wrongs. In short, he is the young peasant hero.

The bald head which gives Keloğlan his name is actually the result of a scalp disease, but such a boy is considered lucky and is envied, rather than pitied. In fact, Keloğlan is so popular a figure that often a prince or princess will assume a Keloğlan disguise in order to achieve remarkable goals.

Whether real or disguised, a Keloğlan is a folk character worth watching, a fine fellow to add to the world's store of heroes. May you enjoy your adventures with Keloğlan in *Once There Was and Twice There Wasn't*.

Barbara K. Walker

Lubbock, Texas

Once There Was and Twice There Wasn't

Turkish Tales Collected by

BARBARA K. WALKER

Illustrated by GORDON KIBBEE

FOLLETT PUBLISHING COMPANY

Chicago  New York

To my daughter,
TERRI SUE,
who never tires
of Turkish tales

Keloğlan and the Ooh-Genie appeared in The Instructor *of March, 1964, in abbreviated form ("Keloğlan and the Three Gifts") and is used with permission.*

Library of Congress Catalog Card Number: 67-21156

First Printing

Follett Publishing Company
1010 West Washington Boulevard Chicago, Illinois 60607

T/L 6540

CONTENTS

Keloğlan

and the Ooh-Genie

Once There Was and twice there wasn't, when genies played polo in the old Turkish bath, when the camel was a salesman and the flea a barber—well, in those days there was a forgetful bald-headed boy named Keloğlan. This Keloğlan lived with his mother in a cottage at the edge of the village, and since their bread and cheese depended on him, they ate but little.

By luck, one day Keloğlan found a five-para piece in the road. On the way home with it, he passed the market, and there he saw a sack of roasted chick-peas. In a moment, he had traded the five paras for some chick-peas. Forgetting that he was on his way home, he started walking toward the river, eating chick-peas all the way. But as he leaned over to look at a fish, he dropped the last of his chick-peas into the water. "Ooh, hoo, hoo, I dropped my chick-peas! I dropped my chick-peas!" he howled, and scratched his bald head and scratched his bald head.

While Keloğlan was howling, the ooh-genie appeared, with his feet on the ground and his turban almost touching the sky. "Oh, bald boy! Why are you howling so?"

Keloğlan said, "Oh, sir, I dropped my chick-peas into the water. Now I haven't any more." And he began again to howl and to scratch his bald head.

"Stop that howling!" the genie ordered. "Here is a five-para piece. Go and get some more chick-peas for yourself."

And off went Keloğlan, with not so much as a word of thanks, to get himself some more chick-peas. He meant to take them home, but in a little while he was back at the river, with only a handful of chick-peas left. As he bent over to watch a fish, the last of his chick-peas fell into the water. "Ooh, hoo, hoo, I dropped my chick-peas! I dropped my chick-peas!" he howled, and scratched his bald head and scratched his bald head.

There came that great big genie again. "Oh,

9

bald boy! Why are you howling so?" he asked.

Keloğlan said, "Oh, sir, I dropped my chick-peas into the water. Now I haven't any more." And he began to howl and to scratch his bald head.

"Stop that noise at once!" the genie demanded. "You should have known better than to drop your chick-peas again. But I have something here that's much better than chick-peas. Take this board home with you. Whenever you put it on the floor and say, 'Spread, my board, spread!' it will spread itself with all sorts of delicious foods. Eat all you want. When you have finished, say, 'Board, fold yourself,' and the rest of the food will disappear. You can keep the board, but this you must remember: Part with your head, but not your secret."

Off went Keloğlan, with not so much as a word of thanks, to see what the board could do. "Mother," he called as he entered the cottage, "come and see what I brought home." Putting the board in the middle of the room, he said, "Spread, my board, spread!" And the words were scarcely spoken when the board became filled with all sorts of delicious

foods—*dolmas* and *böreks* and pilav and baklava—
and Keloğlan and his mother both ate until they
could eat no more. When Keloğlan said, "Board,
fold yourself," the rest of the food disappeared, the
board folded itself, and Keloğlan stood it against
the wall.

From that day on, Keloğlan and his mother lived
so happily that they could scarcely believe their good
fortune. They grew healthy, and even fat, and they
became the talk of the village. But Hasan, the
greedy fellow next door, wondered long and longer
about this change in his neighbors. Meeting Keloğlan one day, he said, "You must have found a bag of
gold somewhere. How else could you be eating
so well?"

Keloğlan, forgetting at first what the genie had
said, answered, "Oh, it's no bag of gold. It's a plain
board that I found."

"A plain board? How can a plain board bring
you food?" Hasan asked.

Noticing the gleam in his neighbor's eye, Keloğlan said, "Ah, that's my secret."

But Hasan had heard all he needed to know. The next day when it came time for dinner, he stood quietly outside Keloğlan's cottage where there was a small crack in the wall, and he watched as Keloğlan put the board in the middle of the room. "Spread, my board, spread!" Keloğlan said, and Hasan could scarcely believe his eyes at the feast which appeared on the board. He watched as Keloğlan and his mother ate. He listened carefully as Keloğlan said, "Board, fold yourself."

"I must have that board for myself," Hasan decided. And he looked and looked until he had found a board that looked exactly like the one Keloğlan had. Then one day, when Keloğlan and his mother had gone to a wedding feast, he slipped into their house and traded his worthless board for Keloğlan's magic one.

The next morning at breakfast time Keloğlan put the board in the middle of the floor and said, "Spread, my board, spread!" But the board didn't spread. Keloğlan repeated, "Spread, my board, spread!" And nothing happened. "Spread, my board, spread!" Keloğlan shouted, but the board lay just like any ordinary board on the floor. Then Keloğlan knew that his own board had been stolen. What would he and his mother do for food?

Keloğlan thought for a while. Then he slipped into his worn shoes and walked to the river. "Ooh, hoo, hoo!" he howled. "Someone has stolen my board. Now how can I live?" And all the while he howled, he scratched his bald head.

Suddenly the great big ooh-genie came again, with his feet on the ground and his turban almost in the sky. "Stop that howling, bald boy!" he ordered. "Of course, someone stole your board. And why wouldn't it be stolen as soon as you told someone about it? Didn't I tell you to part with your head but not your secret?"

"Oh, sir, I forgot," said Keloğlan. "But, ooh, hoo, hoo, my board is gone. And how shall I live?" he howled, scratching and scratching his bald head.

"Stop that howling!" the genie commanded. "You were fool enough to lose your board. But I have something better than a board. Here is a donkey. When you say, 'Give gold, my donkey, give gold!' it will spit out gold pieces. When you have enough gold, say, 'Stop, my donkey, stop!' You can keep the donkey, but remember: Part with your head but not your secret."

Off went Keloğlan, with not so much as a word of thanks, to see what the donkey could do. He led the donkey into their small stable. Then he called, "Mother, come and see what I brought home." As soon as she had come into the stable, Keloğlan closed the door. Then he said, "Give gold, my donkey, give gold!" To their delight, the donkey spat out one gold piece after another, until Keloğlan and his mother could scarcely stuff the coins into the old grain sack at the back of the stable. "Stop, my donkey, stop!" Keloğlan said, and the donkey stopped spitting gold and began to eat the straw in the stall.

14   Now that Keloğlan and his mother had enough gold to make them rich, they decided to live as wealthy, important people. They had a big house built, and they covered the floors with rugs and car-

pets. Instead of their old straw mats, they had fine, soft beds. They dressed themselves in elegantly embroidered clothing. And they killed lambs and gave them to the poor. They became known for their fine living and their generous ways.

Meanwhile, Hasan saw the change that had come about in his neighbors, and he wondered long and longer about it. "How can this be?" he asked himself. "I stole their board, and now they have even better fortune than before. I must find out about this." And one Friday he stopped to chat with Keloğlan after the service at the mosque. "Allah has been good to you, neighbor. How else can one account for such good fortune?"

Forgetting for a moment what the genie had said, Keloğlan laughed. "Well, it might be Allah. But then, again, it might be a donkey!"

"A donkey!" exclaimed Hasan. "How could a donkey make such a change in your life?"

Keloğlan, remembering what had happened to his board, scratched his bald head. "A donkey? Did I say a donkey? The donkey is myself, neighbor. And now, good night." He walked home and carefully covered the window of the stable so that no one could see his donkey.

But Hasan was determined to find the answer to this puzzle. He went around and around Keloğlan's house, and around and around the stable, until finally he found a hole to peep through. Yes, there was a donkey inside—a very ordinary-looking donkey—eating the straw in the stall. Still, the neighbor wasn't satisfied. He watched day after day until he saw both Keloğlan and his mother go into the stable and close the door. Then he hurried over and peeped through a hole in the stable wall. He listened as Keloğlan said, "Give gold, my donkey, give gold!" And he watched in amazement as the donkey spat out gold piece after gold piece, in a great shining heap on the floor. Trembling with eagerness, he watched and listened until he heard Keloğlan say, "Stop, my donkey, stop!" The donkey stopped spitting gold pieces and went back to eating the straw in the stall. As soon as Keloğlan began to stuff the gold pieces into the old grain sack at the back of the stable, Hasan hurried back to his house. Somehow he must manage to get that donkey for himself. But how?

Hasan looked and looked until he had found a donkey exactly like Keloğlan's. Then one day, while Keloğlan and his mother had gone to attend a funeral, he hurried to the stable with his new donkey and exchanged it for Keloğlan's donkey. Quickly he led Keloğlan's donkey to the stable back of his own house and put him into a large stall. "Give gold, my donkey, give gold!" he commanded. And the donkey spat gold pieces until even Hasan was satisfied. "Stop, my donkey, stop!" he said, and while the donkey ate straw, Hasan counted the coins over and over again.

After a while, Keloğlan had used all the gold in his grain sack, and he went one morning to the donkey. "Give gold, my donkey, give gold!" he said. But the donkey just looked at him and went on eating straw. "Give gold, my donkey, give gold!" Keloğlan repeated, more loudly. But the donkey just flicked one ear and went on eating. "Give gold, my donkey, give gold!" Keloğlan shouted, but the donkey stood there, stubborn as any donkey, and not a single gold piece did he spit. So Keloğlan knew that his own donkey had been stolen. "Now what am I to do?" he said. "How shall we eat? How shall we live?"

Keloğlan thought and thought. Then he walked in his fine new shoes to the river. "Ooh, hoo, hoo!" he howled. "Someone has stolen my donkey. Now

18

how can I live? " And all the while he howled, he scratched his bald head and scratched his bald head.

Suddenly that great big ooh-genie came again, with his feet on the ground and his turban almost in the sky. "Stop that howling, bald boy!" he ordered. "Of course, someone stole your donkey. And why wouldn't it be stolen as soon as you told someone about it? Didn't I tell you to part with your head but not your secret?"

"Oh, sir, I forgot," said Keloğlan. "But, ooh, hoo, hoo, my donkey is gone. Now how can I live?" And all the while he howled, he scratched his bald head and scratched his bald head.

"Stop that howling!" the genie commanded. "You've been fool enough to lose your board and your donkey. How do I know that you have learned your lesson?"

"Oh, sir, I have, I have!" Keloğlan cried. "Truly, I'll remember this time!"

"Perhaps this stick of wisdom will help you to remember," said the genie. "I'll give you the stick of wisdom. This is how it works: Beat, my stick, beat!" As soon as the genie had said this, the stick began to beat Keloğlan on his bald head, *putt-ta-kit-ta, putt-ta-kit-ta.*

When Keloğlan had had enough, the genie said, "Stop, my stick, stop!" And the stick stopped beating. "Here, boy, is the stick. Now, look at me. Don't you ever come back here crying and whining again, or I'll finish you! Take your stick to the one you suspect of stealing your board and your donkey. Set the stick to beating him, and let him be beaten until he has learned to leave your things alone. He'll give you back your board and your donkey. Take good care of them! Now, be off about your business."

With not so much as a word of thanks, Keloğlan went home. "Well, Mother, I have a magic something else. Now we'll see what can be done with it to mend our fortunes," said Keloğlan.

20   He took his mother with him and went directly to Hasan. "Look, neighbor," he began. "You stole the board that gave me my food. You stole the donkey that gave me my gold. Will you return

them to me as any honest person should?"

Hasan laughed scornfully. "What board? What donkey? I haven't taken anything of yours."

"Oh, you haven't? We'll just see!" said Keloğlan. "Look. Over there against the wall is a board. Put it down in the middle of the room, and we'll see whether it is mine or not."

Much against his will, Hasan put the board on the floor. "Spread, my board, spread!" ordered Keloğlan, and immediately the board was spread with all kinds of delicious foods. Keloğlan and his mother sat down and ate and ate, until they could eat no more. "Well," said Keloğlan, "the board is mine. Now, let's go out to your stable."

"My stable!" exclaimed Hasan. But he went with Keloğlan and his mother to the donkey's stall. "Give gold, my donkey, give gold!" ordered Keloğlan, and the donkey began to spit gold until there was scarcely room for it in the stall.

21

"Now, neighbor," said Keloğlan. "Will you, or will you not, return these things to me?"

"Indeed, I will not," answered Hasan angrily.

"Why should I? They belong to me."

At that, Keloğlan took the stick from under his jacket. "Beat, my stick, beat!" he commanded, and the stick began to beat Hasan on the head, *putt-ta-kit-ta, putt-ta-kit-ta,* until Hasan had danced himself out of the stable and into the house.

"I'll give you back your things!" he shouted. "But stop that stick!"

"Will you ever take anything of mine again?" asked Keloğlan, as the stick continued to play its tune on Hasan's head.

22

"Never, never!" exclaimed Hasan. "As Allah is my witness, I'll never touch a thing of yours again."

"Stop, my stick, stop!" Keloğlan ordered. Keloğlan loaded the gold on his donkey's back. Then

he took his board and his donkey and his stick, and
he and his mother returned home. From that day
on, they lived in peace and contentment. And may
we all have a share of their luck!

Translated with the aid of Türköz Ozdemir, Ankara, Turkey.

Keloğlan

and the Magician

Once There Was and twice there wasn't, when I was rocking my father's cradle *tungur mungur*—well, in those days there was a clever bald-headed boy named Keloğlan. This Keloğlan had nobody in the world except his mother, but the two of them lived comfortably enough in a little cottage. As for their living, Keloğlan earned that by tending sheep for the people in the village.

When Keloğlan had grown to be a handsome young man, he came to his mother one day and said, "Mother, it is time for me to be married."

"Think, my son! How can you provide for a wife when we two can barely be comfortable on what you earn tending the sheep?"

"Never mind, Mother. We'll manage," Keloğlan answered. "Now, tell me. Isn't it time for me to be married?"

Keloğlan's mother thought this way and that about the matter. Of course, the girl would come to live with them, and she might well be a help around the house. "You may be right, my son. Have you found the one you want to marry?"

"That I have, Mother," said Keloğlan. "I want to marry the padishah's daughter. Who else?"

"Are you out of your mind?" his mother asked. "Surely you do not suppose the padishah will give you his only daughter! Why, they'd laugh me through the gate if I went to ask for her hand for my Keloğlan."

"Never fear, Mother. Some things can be done as well as others. Am I not strong and handsome? Why shouldn't the padishah be willing to give me his daughter? Tomorrow you will please dress yourself nicely and go to the palace to ask for the princess' hand in marriage."

Will she, nill she, Keloğlan's mother must go to the palace, so right after the second prayer the next day she put on her finest dress and shawl and went to the gate of the palace. By a stroke of fortune, the padishah was in good humor, and so he agreed to see her.

"Well, my good woman, what is it that you want?" he asked as she stood trembling before him.

"I— I—" Keloğlan's mother was suddenly speechless with fright.

"Come, come!" the padishah ordered. "What do you want? Tell me quickly."

Keloğlan's mother became even more frightened than before, but she stammered, "My—my padishah, I have a s—son and his name is Keloğlan. And . . . "

"Well? Well? And what? Tell me quickly!"

"Sir, I'll tell you, but I am sure you will be angry. Please don't be too angry with me. And please don't cut off my head!"

The padishah smiled. "Well, then, I'll not be angry with you. Tell me what you want."

28   "Sir, my son Keloğlan looks after the sheep in our village," she began, "and he buys our bread and cheese with the money he earns. Yesterday he told me that he wanted to be married, and the bride he

wants is your daughter. I said, 'Oh, you are just a shepherd. You can't marry the padishah's daughter.' But he said, 'Why not? I am strong and handsome. Why shouldn't I marry the padishah's daughter?' So, sir, I have come to ask, in the name of the Prophet and by the will of God, for the hand of your daughter."

The padishah laughed. "I'm not angry with you. Your son Keloğlan is bold enough to ask for my daughter's hand; I'll give him my daughter, on one condition. He must learn all the tricks of Ali Ghengis."

Surprised by the padishah's answer, the woman hurried home to Keloğlan. "The padishah will give you his daughter," she said, "if you are able to learn all the tricks of Ali Ghengis. The sooner you learn the tricks, the sooner you can marry the princess."

"What could be easier?" Keloğlan answered. "We'll go tomorrow to Ali Ghengis."

This Ali Ghengis was a magician famous for the great number of tricks which he knew. And he was willing to teach these tricks to any young man who wished to learn them. For forty days, he worked to train a young man. At the end of that time, he asked him if he could now do all the tricks of Ali Ghengis. When he replied "yes," the magician took him to a certain cave and killed him.

No young man had ever been able to learn all the tricks of Ali Ghengis and still come back alive to his village. But Keloğlan was determined to marry the padishah's daughter, so the very next morning he and his mother set off to find Ali Ghengis. They went a little; they went far. They traveled over hills and through valleys, picking hyacinths all the way. And at last they met a man.

"What are you doing here?" he asked.

"We are looking for Ali Ghengis," Keloğlan said, "because I want to learn the tricks of Ali Ghengis."

"I am Ali Ghengis," the man answered. "You, old woman, leave your son with me for forty days. On the forty-first day come again to get him."

Keloğlan's mother returned to her village, and Ali Ghengis took Keloğlan to his home. After he had shown Keloğlan the room where he was to sleep, the magician went out again. Now, the magician's wife and daughter had seen Keloğlan, and they decided to help him. As soon as Ali Ghengis had left, his daughter came to Keloğlan. "You must know," she said, "that at the end of the fortieth day my father will ask you whether you have learned his tricks. If you say 'yes,' he will take you to a cave not far from here and kill you. If you say 'no,' he will decide that you are stupid and will let you go home. If you value your life, you must say 'no.' "

"All right," said Keloğlan. "I thank you for your help." And he put the words of the magician's daughter in his pocket, that is, he remembered them.

When Ali Ghengis returned, he began at once to teach Keloğlan his tricks. Day after day they worked, and Keloğlan said nothing, but he noticed much. Of course, he learned the tricks. But at the end of the fortieth day, when Ali Ghengis said, "Well, my son, have you learned all my tricks?"

Keloğlan blinked and said, "Sir?"

"Have you learned all my tricks?"

31

Keloğlan scratched his bald head. "Sir, sometimes I think I have, and sometimes I think I haven't. Perhaps if we worked for another forty days—"

"Stupid boy!" shouted Ali Ghengis. "Forty days I have worked with you, and still you have not learned the tricks of Ali Ghengis. You belong at home with your mother in the village. You have wasted my time."

And the next morning, when Keloğlan's mother came for her son, the magician said in disgust, "Here, take this stupid son of yours. In forty days he has not learned a single one of my tricks. See if you can at least get your bread and cheese from his labors!"

Keloğlan's mother was disappointed, but she said nothing, and the two started back to their village. While they were passing through a forest, they met a group of hunters running after a rabbit.

"Stay here, Mother," Keloğlan said suddenly. "I'm going to become a dog and follow that rabbit. When I bring him down, the men will want to buy me from you. All right, you will sell me for five

pieces of gold. But you must not sell me with the
collar around my neck. If you sell me with my collar, I shall have to remain a dog. Now, remember
what I say!"

In an instant he had become a dog, and off he
went after the rabbit, and caught him.

"Oh, my good woman, is this dog yours?" asked
the head of the hunters.

"Yes. Why do you ask?" she replied.

"We'd like to buy him," the hunter answered.

"He's been with me for years," the woman said.
"I need him to guard my cottage."

"Just any dog will do for guarding a cottage,"
the huntsman insisted. "Come, we will pay you five

33

gold pieces for him."

"Well," said the woman, "you may have him for five pieces of gold. But I must have his collar. I will need it for my new watchdog."

The huntsman removed the collar and counted the five gold pieces into the hand of Keloğlan's mother. Away went the dog after another rabbit, with the hunters hurrying as fast as they could to keep him in sight.

Dodging here and there, Keloğlan came to an open place in the forest, and suddenly he turned into an old man with an axe in his hand. Chunk, chunk, he chopped away at a tree. As he stopped to rest for a minute, there came the chief huntsman, hoo-hooing and hallooing for his dog.

"Old man," he asked, "did you see a dog pass this way?"

The old man scratched his head. "Well, sir, I heard a dog, over there," he said, pointing to the thickest part of the forest. "But he didn't come out into the clearing." The old man returned to his chopping, while the head huntsman and his fellows plunged deep into the forest after their dog.

Meanwhile, Keloğlan's mother had just stooped to take a drink of water from a spring when she heard a sound, and there stood Keloğlan beside her. "Come, Mother," he said, and they started walking toward their own village. As they approached the village, Keloğlan suddenly smiled. "Mother, I am going to become a cow, and you must sell me at the market in our town. Tie a rope around my neck and lead me there. Sell me for ten gold pieces. But there is one thing you must remember. Be sure to take the rope from my neck before you give me to my new owner. If you do not, I shall have to remain a cow."

Before Keloğlan's mother had time to blink once, there stood a fine cow before her, with a rope on the ground nearby. She tied the rope carefully around the cow's neck and began to lead it along the path to town. Before long, they arrived at the small marketplace, and she stood with the other peasants waiting to sell fruits and vegetables and animals.

Now, Ali Ghengis had been thinking about Keloğlan all this time. "Perhaps Keloğlan has deceived me," he said to himself. "I must find out where he is and what he is doing." In the flicker of an eyelid, Ali Ghengis appeared in the marketplace of Keloğlan's town, where he saw Keloğlan's mother with a cow. The magician recognized the woman, but how could she know that the bearded cowherd who came to buy her cow was the magician?

"Good woman," Ali Ghengis began, "that is a

fine cow. How much are you asking for her?"

"I want ten pieces of gold," replied the woman.

"Suppose I give you twenty pieces of gold? That would be more than fair," Ali Ghengis offered. "But I must have the rope with the cow, since I will need to lead her home."

When Keloğlan's mother heard "twenty pieces of gold," her son's warning about the rope flew clean out of her head. "Of course," she said, and she held the end of the rope out toward Ali Ghengis.

Keloğlan, realizing that things were not going at all as he had planned, suddenly turned himself into a small bird and began to fly here and there, and then out of the marketplace. No sooner had he taken wing than Ali Ghengis became a hawk, and started in pursuit of him. Keloğlan had just reached the padishah's palace when he saw the hawk above him, ready to pounce. Changing suddenly into a red rose, Keloğlan fell through the princess' window.

"Oh!" cried the princess. "What a beautiful rose!" and she breathed its fragrance with delight. "Look, Father," she said, holding the rose out the window to show it to the padishah, who was walking in the garden. "A bird must have brought me this flower. It's different from all the roses in your garden."

Suddenly there came a knock at the garden gate,

and when a servant opened it, there stood a beggar. "Oh, sir," he said, addressing the padishah. "As you can see, I am very poor. Just a few moments ago, I traded my last loaf of bread for a red rose, thinking that if I must die of hunger, I might well die with beauty in my hand. Suddenly a bird swooped down and took my rose, and carried it to your palace, dropping it through a window. Have you seen it?"

The padishah thought for a minute. Of course, that must be the rose his daughter had shown him. "Daughter," he called. "Come to the garden."

Down came the princess, as beautiful as the fourteenth day of the moon, with the rose laid softly at her cheek.

"That's it!" the beggar exclaimed. "That's my rose! May I have it?"

"Oh, no," the princess said. "This is my rose." And she breathed deeply of the glowing flower.

"My daughter," the padishah said firmly, "the rose belongs to this man. You must give it to him."

At last the girl held the rose toward the beggar, who was reaching eagerly for it when all at once it fell to the ground as gleaming grains of wheat. In a flash, the beggar became a chicken, and started to peck at the wheat. Here and there he hurried on little, mincing feet, eating the grains which had been scattered across the grass.

Just as he was reaching for the last grain, it turned into a fox and gobbled him up. And that was the last of Ali Ghengis.

40

"Are we dreaming?" asked the padishah. "What is all this?"

As he and his daughter stood puzzling over this strange turn of affairs, the fox became a handsome young man. "My padishah," he said, "my name is Keloğlan. When my mother came to ask for your daughter's hand in marriage, you said that first I must learn all the tricks of Ali Ghengis. I learned them well, for the chicken you just saw eaten by the fox was Ali Ghengis himself. Now I am the only one who knows all the tricks of Ali Ghengis, and I have come for your daughter."

Never had the padishah thought so quickly. If he did not keep the promise he had made, he decided, Keloğlan might well play an Ali Ghengis trick on him. Besides, the fellow was strong and handsome, and the princess would have good reason to be pleased with him.

"My daughter is yours," he said. "Let the wedding ceremonies begin at once."

The wedding was a fine one, lasting forty days and forty nights. They went to live in the palace, of course. And Keloğlan and the princess lived in peace and contentment all their days.

41

Adapted from a story told by Dikmen Gürün, Istanbul, Turkey.

Keloğlan

and the Magic Hairs

Once There Was and twice there wasn't, in the old days, when the camel was town crier and I was rocking my father's cradle *tungur mungur*— well, in those days there was a bald-headed boy named Keloğlan.

This Keloğlan had two older brothers whose chief delight was to see their youngest brother run about on errands. "Keloğlan, sweep out the stable," the first would order. And, "Carry some water, you lazy thing," the second would roar. "Now curry the horses," the first would demand, before Keloğlan had even caught his breath from bringing the water. Despite the abuse from his brothers, the boy remained good-natured, fetching and carrying as fast as his legs could trot.

44

One day as Keloğlan was hurrying back from the village fountain, he heard the town crier making a most interesting announcement. "Hear ye all the word of the padishah! The padishah's lovely daughter has promised to marry the horseman skillful enough to perform a certain task. Come, ye, all who would try for the hand and heart of the princess! On Monday next, come ye all to the padishah's palace for the contest. Hear ye! Hear ye!"

"Did you hear the town crier?" Keloğlan asked his brothers as he set down the water jars.

"Of course, stupid boy," one answered. "Who could miss the news? I suppose you think you are the horseman skillful enough to win the princess?" And the brothers shook with laughter at the very idea.

"I'd never win the princess, but I'd like to see the contest," Keloğlan admitted. "If you're going to watch the horsemen, could I go along with you?"

"Ha! What would you do there? If skill could be gained by watching, every dog would become a butcher!" And the older brothers sent him off to prepare their clothes for the event.

But on Monday, after Keloğlan had saddled

45

his brothers' horses and seen them off for the padishah's palace, he decided to go himself. Reaching into the pocket of his shabby trousers, he pulled
out three hairs, a white one, a brown one, and a
black one.

"The old man who gave me these hairs said that
if I rubbed the white hair, a white horse would appear, and with the white horse a white suit and a
turban for me to wear," murmured Keloğlan. "Well,
there's nothing to be lost by trying!" and he rubbed
the white hair between his thumb and forefinger.
Phut! There stood a beautiful white horse, and on
its back was a handsome white suit and a turban.
Putting the hairs back into his pocket, Keloğlan
donned the white suit and the turban, mounted the
white horse, and stirred the dust into great clouds as
he rode to the padishah's palace, arriving there before
his brothers.

46   The padishah's daughter, lovely as the fourteenth day of the moon, set the task. "The horseman
who will win my hand must leap the ravine behind
my father's palace," she announced. "How easy!"

whispered one. "How fair!" answered another. And the handsomest, bravest young men of the kingdom vied for the chance to be first. But, alas, the ravine was wider than they had judged, and one after another they met defeat. Suddenly Keloğlan rode up to the starting place, pressed his horse forward with great, bounding leaps, and cleared the ravine with a handsome margin to spare.

"The young man on the white horse has won the hand of the princess!" In ringing tones, the padishah's own crier made the announcement.

But where was the victor? Here and there and everywhere a search was made for the winner, but he had disappeared—both he and his horse had simply vanished. At last a new announcement was made: "Tomorrow there will be a second contest for the hand of the padishah's daughter. Hear ye! Hear ye!" The crowd dispersed, marveling at this unusual turn of events.

47

Meanwhile, Keloğlan had returned home, dismissing the white horse, on whose back he placed the white suit and the turban. He cheerfully unsaddled his brothers' horses when they arrived. "How was the contest?" he asked as he rubbed the steaming horses.

"Oh, even you would have enjoyed it," his older brother said. "Think of it! A fine gentleman on a white horse almost flew across the ravine."

"Then he won the hand of the princess?"

"Oh, no, for he disappeared as soon as the contest was finished," answered the other. "Since he did not come to claim the prize, there is to be another contest tomorrow for the hand of the padishah's daughter."

"How I wish I could see it!" Keloğlan sighed.

"Well, next time we'll take you, if you'll promise not to make fools of us all," the brothers agreed.

And on Tuesday, after Keloğlan had saddled his brothers' horses, he was allowed to saddle one for himself, a wretched beast that could barely put one hoof before the other. In no time at all, the two older brothers had ridden far ahead of Keloğlan, laughing all the while at that foolish fellow on his sorry steed. As soon as his brothers were out of

48

sight, Keloğlan slipped off his horse's back and tied him securely to an olive tree. Reaching into his pocket, he took out the three hairs, and, deciding on the brown one, he rubbed it between his thumb and forefinger. *Phut!* There stood a beautiful brown horse; on its back a handsome brown suit and a turban for him to wear. Slipping the hairs back into his pocket, Keloğlan donned the brown suit and the turban, mounted the brown horse, and was off in a great cloud of dust for the padishah's palace, arriving there before his brothers.

This time the padishah's daughter ordered that the contestants leap an even wider part of the ravine. Again, after the other horsemen had tried and failed, Keloğlan came riding up on his brown horse, took a flying start, and leaped the ravine with an even wider margin to spare.

"The young man on the brown horse has won the hand of the princess!" In ringing tones, the padishah's own crier made the announcement.

49

Again the victor had disappeared, and the hand of the princess went unclaimed. After a hasty con-

ference of the padishah with his viziers, another announcement was made: "Tomorrow there will be a third contest for the hand of the padishah's daughter. Hear ye! Hear ye!" and the crowd went its way, with much talk about the remarkable horseman.

In the meantime, Keloğlan had returned to the olive tree where he had left the old horse. He took off the brown suit and the turban. Dismissing the brown horse, Keloğlan mounted the horse his brothers had chosen for him, and rode slowly toward the padishah's palace. Before long, he met his brothers, returning in a white heat down the road.

"Turn around! There's no need to go farther," his older brother shouted. And obediently Keloğlan turned his horse around and hobbled toward home. By the time he arrived, his brothers had already unsaddled their horses and were rubbing them down. "At the rate you rode home, we could have unsaddled forty horses," the younger one scolded. But they told him all about the contest, anyway.

"How I wish I could have seen it!" Keloğlan said wistfully.

"Never mind. There'll be another contest tomorrow, and perhaps you'll ride fast enough next time to get there before the affair is over!"

Both brothers agreed that Keloğlan should have a better horse the following day, so on Wednesday after the boy had saddled the other two horses, he saddled and mounted his own, and they rode off together. Still, the horse was an old one, and before long his brothers had ridden clear out of sight, impatient to see the contest.

Slipping from his horse's back, Keloğlan tied the scrawny beast to a poplar tree. Taking the three hairs from his pocket, he chose the black one, and rubbed it between his thumb and forefinger. *Phut!* There stood a gleaming black horse, and with it a fine black suit and a turban for Keloğlan to wear. Donning the black suit and the turban and mounting his black horse was the work of but a moment or two. Then, in a great cloud of dust, Keloğlan rode off for the padishah's palace, arriving there well before his brothers.

This time the padishah's daughter had arranged

a high hurdle for the horsemen to jump. And this time, resolved that the victor should claim his prize, she had hidden two women behind the hurdle with red stamps in their hands. When a horseman had succeeded in jumping the hurdle, the women were to stamp him on each side of his forehead so that later he could be identified. Again, one contestant after another tried the task and failed. Finally Keloğlan

came riding up on the black horse. Urging his horse forward, he bounded over the hurdle so easily that another horseman could have cleared the hurdle beneath him. The two women were ready for him,

however, and as he landed they quickly stamped each side of his forehead with the bold red seal of the padishah's daughter.

Again the victor disappeared, but this time the

princess was determined to find him. After a hasty conference of the padishah with his viziers, the padishah's crier made a new announcement: "Tomorrow, every man in the kingdom will come to the palace to be viewed by the princess."

"Every man?" "What is the princess looking for?" "How will she know?" Questions of all kinds buzzed among the crowd, for, of course, no one but the princess and the two women knew about the stamps that had been put on the forehead of the remarkable horseman.

When the two brothers returned home, they found Keloğlan waiting for them in the stable, with his head all bandaged.

"What happened to you?" one asked.

"Oh," replied Keloğlan, "I was hurrying toward the padishah's palace, and I fell off my horse and hit my head on a stone."

His wounded head did not excuse him from unsaddling and rubbing down the horses, however. Keloğan set to work, listening with interest as his brothers almost in a single voice told him of the contest. "And," the older one finished, "tomorrow every man in the kingdom is to appear at the padishah's palace to be viewed by the princess."

"Whatever for?" Keloğlan was curious.

"Who knows? Perhaps she hopes to find the gentleman who rode the black horse. At any rate, we must all go, stupid as it seems to take you with us. If the padishah's crier said 'every man,' he doubtless meant even Keloğlans!" said the younger brother.

Thus it was that Keloğlan went with his brothers the next day to the padishah's palace, arriving later than the rest and falling into line at the very end. Man after man was examined, but none bore the red seal of the princess. Suddenly looking up, the padishah's daughter saw a young man with his head bandaged. "Bring that man to me," she ordered, and her attendants went immediately to Keloğlan and led him to the princess.

"Unwrap your head," she demanded. And when Keloğlan had removed the bandage, there was his bald head shining in the sun—and there were the

54

two bold red marks of the princess' seal.

"A Keloğlan!" laughed all who saw. "Surely that *Keloğlan* has not won the daughter of the padishah! There must be some mistake."

But the princess knew the secret of the red seal, and—bald or not—this young man had won her hand. "Why did you hide, when you had earned the right to marry me?" she asked.

"I am just a Keloğlan, and not worthy to be your husband," replied the boy, in a voice little louder than a whisper.

"A man is judged by his work. And, Keloğlan or no Keloğlan, your great skill as a horseman won you the prize. Nothing was said of hair or beard, or fine manners or famous name."

Then the padishah's daughter presented Keloğlan to her father and his viziers. And soon after, Keloğlan married the padishah's daughter, with a wedding celebration that lasted forty day and forty nights.

55

Adapted from a story told by Suzan Koraltürk, Trabzon, Turkey.

Keloğlan

the Kindhearted

Once There Was and twice there wasn't, when the sieve was in the hay, and when genies played polo in the old Turkish bath—well, in those times there was a kindhearted bald-headed boy named Keloğlan.

This Keloğlan lived with his mother in a small hut near the forest, and it was a fine piece of luck that they had a good donkey. For every morning Keloğlan took the donkey into the forest while he cut firewood. And every afternoon he loaded the little donkey with the firewood he had cut, and led him to the marketplace. There he sold the wood to buy bread and cheese for the household and straw for the patient gray donkey.

One afternoon on the way to market Keloğlan came upon some children throwing stones at a dog. "Why are you throwing stones at the dog?" he asked.

"It's a fine little dog, and would grow up to be very useful. Don't throw stones at it. Why don't you give it to me, instead?"

The children laughed at first, and then they looked at each other. This Keloğlan might be willing to exchange something for the worthless beast. "All right," said the leader, "if you'll give us all the wood on your donkey's back, we'll give you the dog."

Keloğlan had worked hard for the wood, but the dog was such a timid little fellow that he couldn't see him abused. "Fine," said he, and he unloaded the wood and took the dog home to his mother.

"Son, what are you doing, bringing home another mouth for us to feed?" cried his mother. Quickly Keloğlan explained what had happened, and his mother, long accustomed to her son's tender heart, sighed and set about preparing their meager supper, while Keloğlan made a little cage for the dog. Every day he fed it, and it grew strong and healthy. 59

Some months later, as Keloğlan was going toward the marketplace, he came upon the same group of children stoning a kitten. "The poor thing!" cried

Keloğlan. "Why are you throwing stones at it? Give it to me, instead, and I'll take good care of it."

The children, remembering the fine bargain they had made with Keloğlan before, decided that this was too good an opportunity to lose. "All right," said one of them, "give us all the wood on your donkey's back, and we'll give you the kitten."

After just a moment's thought of his hard work, Keloğlan exchanged the firewood for the kitten, and he went home to his mother without the bread and cheese they needed. It's said that a hungry stomach has no ears, but Keloğlan's mother, will she, nill she, heard the story of the kitten, and they all went hungry to their beds that night. As for Keloğlan, he was happy, for hadn't he a fine kitten in the little cage he had made for it? As he fed the kitten, day after day, it grew to be a fine, strong cat.

Again, some months later, as Keloğlan was returning with his wood from the forest, he happened upon the same children abusing a small snake. "What a beautiful snake!" he exclaimed. "See it, all slim and colorful, and with its tiny red tongue

60

darting in and out! How can you bear to hurt it?"

The children just laughed. "I suppose," the leader jeered, "you'd like to have the snake, too! Well, give us your firewood and you may have the snake." And they watched to see whether the foolish fellow would make such a bad bargain as that one.

Keloğlan hesitated not at all as he unloaded the firewood. Then he reached cautiously for the baby snake and carried him home to his mother. "What are we going to do with a snake, my son?" This last exchange was almost too much for his mother. "We have a cat and a dog, and now a snake. What can be the use of a snake?"

"Never mind, Mother," Keloğlan said. "Since the cat and the dog have grown so strong and healthy, we can let them run about and find their own food. They'll surely stay nearby, since we've fed them so long. And then we'll have only the snake to care for." So saying, the boy opened the cages, *61* and out ran the dog and the cat. Thankless creatures, the two ran in opposite directions. Keloğlan waited, but they didn't return.

"You see, my boy? What good did it do to feed them?" his mother asked. "Why bother with the snake? It is even more useless than those other two!" But Keloğlan felt sorry for the slim young thing, and put it in a cage and cared for it day after day.

One afternoon, as he was feeding the snake, Keloğlan was startled to hear it speak to him. "Oh, master, please take me home to my family. My father and mother live beneath the roots of the largest hazelnut bush in the forest, and they are surely grieving for me."

After he had recovered from his surprise, Keloğlan replied, "I'd be happy to take you home, but, after all, your parents are snakes, and how do I know that they wouldn't kill me?"

"No, they won't," said the snake, "because this is what you are going to do: Put me in a *chanta*. Take me to my father and mother, and when you come near the hazelnut bush, I'll stick my head out of the *chanta*. When they see me alive and safe, they'll be so thankful that they will not kill you. But, remember, when they ask you what you want as a reward for my return, be sure to ask for my father's gold ring."

Keloğlan placed the snake in his mother's *chanta* and went directly to the hazelnut bush. As the snake's father and mother coiled to strike at the boy, the young snake raised his head above the edge of the *chanta* and greeted them. His parents were so happy to see their lost one that they led Keloğlan at once to their home beneath the bush and made him welcome indeed.

After a long conversation, the father snake said

63

courteously, "Wish from me whatever you want."

And just as courteously, Keloğlan replied, "My friend, I wish only your good health."

Again the snake's father said, "Come, wish of me whatever you want."

And once again Keloğlan answered, "My friend, I wish only your good health."

For the third time, the snake's father said, "Thank you, my friend, but my health is for me. Come, wish from me whatever you want for yourself."

This time, Keloğlan said, "If I wished anything for myself, it would be your gold ring."

Immediately the father snake removed the plain gold ring from his tail, and Keloğlan thanked him and slipped it on his finger. After bidding them good-bye, he started for home.

On his way home, he became very dusty from the wheels of a passing oxcart, and he flicked the dust carefully from his shoulders. As the ring touched his shoulder, a flame darted out, and a voice said, "Wish from me whatever you want."

Marveling, Keloğlan said, "I am very hungry. I should like some food." And suddenly there appeared before him a tray laden with all sorts of delicious foods. Eagerly Keloğlan seated himself on the ground and ate until he was satisfied. Then he went on until he reached home.

That evening, as he sat talking with his mother about this and that, he said, "Mother, I'd like to marry, and I believe I'll marry the padishah's older daughter. Please arrange a wedding for us."

His mother gasped. "Oh, my son, the padishah would never give you his older daughter as a bride!"

"Perhaps, and perhaps not," said the boy. "I rather think he will. At any rate, please go tomorrow and ask."

And the very next day, Keloğlan's mother went to the gate of the padishah's palace to ask for the princess' hand for her bald-headed boy. Of course, the servants at the gate jeered at the woman in her tattered dress, and she returned, saddened but not at all surprised, to her own little hut. "You see?" she said. "They wouldn't even let me in!"

Several days passed, but Keloğlan had not forgotten the padishah's older daughter. One night as he lay in bed, the boy licked the ring on his finger, and a great genie appeared, with his slippers on the floor and his turban touching the ceiling. "Wish from me whatever you want."

Immediately Keloğlan said, "I wish for my mother a dress more beautiful than any owned by the padishah's two daughters, and I wish it ready by tomorrow morning."

Sure enough, in the morning there was a dress more beautiful than anyone could even imagine, with a pair of fine slippers to match. Keloğlan's mother put on the dress and slippers and went directly to the padishah's palace. This time, she was invited to enter. At length she saw the padishah and asked for the hand of his older daughter for her son Keloğlan.

"Keloğlan, eh?" mused the king. "Well, your bald-headed boy may have my older daughter on one condition: by tomorrow morning he must build for her a palace as fine as mine, for my daughter is accustomed to comfort and splendor." And he smiled behind his hand as the woman left. What a ridiculous proposal!

Grieved, Keloğlan's mother returned home and told her son the result of her errand.

"What could be easier, Mother?" he replied. That evening, Keloğlan licked the ring again. Again the genie appeared, with his slippers on the floor and his turban touching the ceiling, and said, "Wish from me whatever you want."

"I wish to have a palace built, one more grand and more beautiful than the padishah's palace, and

it must be built by morning."

And what do you think! In the morning there stood a beautiful palace, gleaming in the sun, and of course the padishah had to give his older daughter to Keloğlan. After their wedding had been celebrated, Keloğlan and his bride went to live in the new palace.

Now, in truth, though Keloğlan had wanted his bride, she had not wanted him at all, for she had already found a sweetheart of her own. Sly thing that she was, she determined somehow or other to keep the palace but to get rid of her bald husband. One evening after she had pretended to fall asleep, she saw Keloğlan lick the ring and demand of the genie a fine new carriage for his wife. "Aha!" she thought, "so *that* is how he built the palace . . . ." And she resolved to make the ring her own.

A few days later, as Keloğlan was about to take a journey, she pouted and sulked and wouldn't be comforted. At last she smiled prettily and said, "If you won't take me with you, at least leave me something to comfort me while you are gone—something small, but your own. That plain ring on your finger would do."

"Oh, no," he answered. "The ring wouldn't do at all."

But she sulked and pouted, and even hinted that if he didn't love her enough to give her a plain old ring, she'd run away to someone who loved her more. At length, Keloğlan had had enough of her fretfulness, and he took the ring from his finger and slipped it alongside her wedding ring. Meekly she kissed him good-bye, and off he went, happy that he had been able to please her.

He was barely out of sight when the deceitful girl licked the ring. As soon as the genie had said, "Wish from me whatever you want," she said, "Bring to me my sweetheart, who lives in the small house nearest the village fountain, and transport my husband Keloğlan to a lonely place beyond seven mountains!"

In a moment, there stood the sweetheart, while Keloğlan, to his surprise, found himself in a desert far from the place he had intended to go. Keloğlan, clever fellow that he was, needed no one to tell him that his wife had found the secret of the ring, and quite clearly now he recognized the trickery by which she had secured it. "She is no wife for me!" he decided. "And I must recover the ring. But first I have a journey to make." And he traveled six months and a summer, straight over rivers and dales, picking hyacinths all the way, until at last he came again to his own village.

To his surprise, the new palace was no longer there. And what had become of it? The wily girl had licked the ring again and had commanded the genie to transport the palace to an island some distance out in the sea, where Keloğlan could not find her. There she and her sweetheart had celebrated a wedding of their own, and were living a rich, full life.

Sadly, Keloğlan returned to his old cottage, and he was just telling his mother the whole story when he heard a scratching sound at the door. Opening it, he found to his surprise and joy that the cat and the dog had returned.

Stepping outside, the boy welcomed them, and

70

they in turn asked him how matters were going with him. By this time, Keloğlan had despaired of re-covering the ring, but nonetheless he told the two everything that had happened since they had run away.

"Well," said the cat, "it's not as impossible as you think. I have heard that the palace has been transported to an island some distance off the coast. If I could only swim there, I could steal the ring for you."

"I can swim," offered the dog. "Come, Cat. I'll carry you on my back, and you can recover the ring."

When the two had landed on the island, the cat cautioned the dog to lie quietly out of sight while she scaled the wall to the princess' room. Reassured by the slow breathing of the sleeping girl and her sweetheart, the cat explored the room, but the ring was nowhere to be found. Suddenly, as the girl turned in her sleep, there was a clicking noise against her teeth, and the cat realized that the ring must be hidden in the girl's mouth. It was the matter of

71

but a moment for the cat to leap softly to the pillow and lay her furry tail across the girl's nose. Opening her mouth to breathe, the girl revealed the ring, which the cat deftly scooped up in her paw and popped into her own mouth. Hurriedly returning to the dog, the cat showed him the ring, and the two started back to Keloğlan, who was waiting for them on the shore nearest the island.

Halfway across the water, the dog began to feel jealous that his companion was carrying the ring. "Here," he said, "let me carry the ring for a while.

I'm doing all the work of carrying you, and I should have a chance to carry the ring."

"Don't be foolish," retorted the cat. "You have enough to do with your swimming. Besides, I stole the ring, didn't I? I have the better right to carry it first. When we reach the shore, you can carry it."

The dog swam on, but the closer he came to the shore, the crosser he became about the whole matter. "If you don't give me the ring at once, I'll overturn you into the water, and you can swim ashore yourself with the ring," said he. Fearing for her life, the cat reached out to place the ring in the dog's mouth, but, alas, it slipped from her paw and went down, down, down into the sea.

"Now look at what's happened!" the cat exclaimed. Immediately they both looked anxiously here and there for the ring, but it was nowhere in sight. As they looked, they noticed several fishermen pulling ashore, their boats filled to the gunwales with fish. "Aha!" said the cat. "Perhaps a fish has swallowed the ring. Let's ask the fishermen for some fish."

"Please, fishermen," began the dog as he and the cat came on shore, "could you spare us a fish or two?"

"Oh, yes, please, sirs," added the cat. "We are so hungry!"

The fishermen were so surprised and amused to hear a cat and a dog speaking that they threw one small fish after another to them as they went about the business of sorting and packing their catch for market. As fast as they could move, the cat and the dog set to work on the heap of fish accumulating at their feet. Were they eating them? Oh, no! Eagerly they were opening up the stomach of each fish, looking for the ring they had lost through their foolish quarrel. At last, in the stomach of the very last fish they found it. Quickly the cat popped the ring into her mouth, and the two companions ran directly to Keloğlan.

74 As soon as the cat had dropped the ring at her master's feet, the boy picked it up and licked it. There came that great genie again, with his slippers on the ground and his turban almost touching the

clouds. "Wish from me whatever you want," said he.

"Take me and my companions at once to the padishah's palace," ordered Keloğlan, and in an instant the three found themselves in the audience chamber of the padishah.

"Well!" exclaimed the king. "What have we here?" As he and his court marveled at the sudden reappearance of Keloğlan, the boy told of the deceitful behavior of the padishah's older daughter. "Sire," concluded Keloğlan, "I am sorry I ever asked for your daughter's hand."

"And I am sorry to have fathered such a daughter!" the padishah answered. "Since she has done you such an injustice and has brought upon me such disgrace, what punishment do you feel would be a just one for her? Death for her and her sweetheart?" For the padishah feared the power and wrath of this unusual Keloğlan, and hoped to make his peace with him.

As Keloğlan hesitated, thinking the matter over, he noticed the girl, beautiful as the fourteenth day

75

of the moon, sitting near the padishah. As Keloğlan gazed at her, the girl blushed and looked down, but her pleasing smile had given the boy a fine new idea. "Sire," said he, "I had planned to marry a padishah's daughter. If your younger daughter's hand is not promised, what would you say to our being married?

76   Your older daughter might then be welcome to her sweetheart. With a punishment no worse than that, we might all be content!"

A glance at his smiling daughter told the padishah that this would indeed be a splendid solution, so soon afterwards Keloğlan and the padishah's younger daughter were married, with a wedding celebration that lasted forty days and forty nights. After the celebration, Keloğlan and his new bride moved into a palace even larger and more beautiful than the one he had ordered for his first bride, and since the padishah's younger daughter had loved Keloğlan from the very beginning, the two lived happily there forever after.

They had their wish fulfilled. Let's go up and sit in their seats!

Adapted from a story told by Ayse Güldemir, Ankara, Turkey.

Keloğlan

and God's Greatness

Once There Was and twice there wasn't, when God's creatures were many and it was a sin to talk too much—well, in those times there was a padishah who was a very proud man, and this padishah had just one daughter. One day as he stood with his daughter on the balcony overlooking his city and a part of his kingdom, he said, "Tell me, my daughter. Is there anyone greater than I am?"

"Why, yes, my father," the girl answered. "God is greater than you are."

"Oh, no, my daughter," said he. And he was angry.

He asked again, another day, "Daughter, tell me. Is anyone greater than I am?"

And he was angry when she answered, again, "Why, yes, my father. God is greater than you are."

For still a third time, he asked, "Come, my

daughter. Tell me. Is anyone greater than I am?"

"God, my father, is greater than you are." And the girl would not change her mind.

Angered beyond measure, the padishah looked around for some means to punish his daughter. *"Simi-i-t! Simi-i-t!"* he heard. And there, passing below them on the street was a poor *simit* seller, with his box of *simits* balanced on his head as he cried his wares. "Aha!" thought the padishah. "There is the answer to my problem." And he called a servant to him. "Go and call that *simit* seller, and tell him to come here."

Quickly the servant stopped the biscuit seller. "Come in right away," he ordered. "The padishah wants you."

Well, the *simit* seller trembled and wrung his hands. "I haven't done anything wrong. Please don't take me there," he begged.

"Whether you have done wrong or right," said the servant, "you are asked by the padishah to go to his side, and you must come."

The poor fellow left his *simit* box by the side of

81

the stairs and *patur kitur patur kitur* went upstairs to the padishah. And as the padishah heard the footsteps, he turned to his daughter and smiled. "Now, my daughter, since you are so sure that God is greater than I, we'll just put you into the hands of God. Surely only God's greatness can help you if you are married to a *simit* seller!"

Stunned, the girl watched as the ragged young man came out onto the balcony. "Here I am, your majesty," he almost whispered, taking off his padded cap as he spoke. "What do you wish?"

"A Keloğlan!" exclaimed the king, as the cap came off and revealed the *simit* seller's bald head. "This is even better than I had hoped!" And he struck his hand against his thigh in satisfaction as he said, "You are just the man I have been looking for as a husband for my daughter. And you are to marry her this very day and take her away with you."

82

"Oh, your Majesty, how can that be?" protested the *simit* seller. "How can I take your daughter as my wife? I am a poor man, with no place to live and little or nothing to eat."

"Nothing could be better for my daughter," answered the padishah. "It is mine to command and yours to obey. Go at once to find a *hoca*, and bring him back to perform your marriage ceremony. Then take my daughter's hand and go away wherever you will."

Keloğlan went down the stairs and out into the street. Who would have thought that such misfortune could befall him? "God finds a low branch for the bird that cannot fly," he murmured. "Perhaps somehow we can manage. At any rate, I must first find a *hoca*." And at length he saw a *hoca* coming from the mosque. "Oh, please, sir," Keloğlan said. "Will you come with me? I have some business for you to perform."

The *hoca* went with Keloğlan to the padishah's balcony, where the marriage ceremony was speedily performed. And just as the padishah had ordered, the boy took his bride by the hand and they started on their way, stopping only while he balanced the *simit* box on his head.

Thinking this way and that, Keloğlan remem-

83

bered a good friend of his who was an innkeeper. "We'll go to my friend," he said gently to the girl, "and see if he will take us in." And they walked through the dusty street to a small inn at the edge of town. "Please, my friend," he began as the innkeeper came to meet him, "I have a wife now, and I have no place for us to stay. Could you let me use a room in the inn? I'll pay you what I can for it, and somehow I'll make it right with you."

"Once a friend, always a friend," responded the innkeeper warmly. "Of course, I'll find you a room. It's a simple room, but you will have shelter there. Come." And he led them down the hall to a small room as bare as it could be. There was no bed— only a straw mat on the floor. There was not even a glass to drink a drop of water. But it was indeed better than no room at all, so Keloğlan left his bride there, locking the door for her safety, and he went out to sell his *simits*. He worked very hard—how he worked!—to sell all his *simits*. Just at sundown, he bought a loaf of bread, some olives, and a little cheese, and came home to eat.

Day after day passed in much the same fashion. If Keloğlan had enough money to add something to their simple fare, he did. If he did not have enough money, they just sat down and ate bread, and they never complained.

Finally he saw that selling *simits* was not enough to make life possible for the two of them, and he said to his wife, "I'll exchange my *simit* box for a stout rope and become a porter. Maybe I shall earn more money for us that way." And he began carrying things for people—big baskets and boxes and all kinds of furniture—and little by little, as his work became known, he made a bit more money. He was able to buy a mattress for them and a rug for the floor and a little kettle to cook in—plain and simple things—a pitcher, and two glasses to drink from, and a little better food to eat. And all this time he was giving some money to the innkeeper, too, saying, "Please excuse me for not being able to pay you regularly."

The innkeeper always answered, "It doesn't matter. I feel you are my brother and she is my sister."

One day a band of merchants stopped at the inn. They were on their way to Baghdad to buy goods and bring them back, but they were unable to start until they could find a strong porter to handle their goods. Seeing a fine opportunity for his friend, the innkeeper suggested, "Why don't you take the porter we call Keloğlan? He's strong and willing, and he's a good man." After conferring among themselves, the merchants agreed to hire him.

Then the innkeeper called Keloğlan to him. "Here is a chance for you, my friend. If you go to Baghdad with these merchants, you'll earn a great deal of money."

"As you say," agreed Keloğlan, "it is a fine job. But you know how it is with me. I have a wife, and I earn my bread daily. If I leave her and go away, she'll have nothing to eat. If the merchants would give me some money in advance, I could leave it with her so that she could have enough to eat while I am gone."

At this, the innkeeper said, "Don't worry. She's like a sister to me, and I'll take good care of her."

Learning of Keloğlan's situation, however, the merchants gave the boy some money to leave for his wife, and then they went on their way, taking him with them as their head porter. They went a little; they went far. They went straight over rivers and over dales. For six months and a summer they went, until they found themselves in a desert. It was hot—oh, it was hot!—and there was no water and no rest.

When they had become desperate, they discovered a well in the desert at the very bottom of which was water. "Let's tie a rope around the waist of one of the porters," said the chief merchant, "and let him down into the well to send up some water for us." And one of the porters was lowered into the well.

But as he went lower into the well, the porter began to scream, "Oh, I am burning! I'm burning!" So they pulled him out.

Another porter said, "Let me try it. I can do it." They tied a rope around his waist and let him down into the well. But when he was part of the way down, he started screaming, "I'm freezing! I'm freezing! It's—take me out! I'm freezing!" So they took him out.

Finally the merchants called Keloğlan aside. "The others haven't been able to do it, and we must have water, or else we and our animals will die. Only you can save us. Let us tie the rope around your waist and let you down into the well."

"But don't you see how dangerous it is?" said Keloğlan. "One went down and said he was burning; the other said he was freezing. There is something very strange about this well. What if I get burned or frozen, and die? What will my wife do without me? If I die, will you promise to pay some compensation to my wife?"

"Yes, yes," agreed the merchants. And, anxious about the well, the chief merchant gave him a bag full of gold. Opening the bag, Keloğlan poured the coins into a big belt and gave it back to him, saying, "In case I am killed, please send this to my wife." Then they tied the rope around his waist and let him down into the well. Soon he began to shout,

"I'm burning, I'm burning!" But they continued to lower him into the well. In a few minutes, he began to shout, "I'm freezing, I'm freezing!" but they still lowered him, until he came to the very bottom, where the precious water lay.

"Send down the buckets!" he called, and they sent the buckets down. One after another, he filled them and they pulled them back up. He filled and they pulled, he filled and they pulled, and the water came up. They drank—oh, how eagerly they drank! And then they had the animals drink all the water they wanted, and they poured the cooling water all around the tents. Finally they said, "We have enough. Come up!"

"Let me have a drink before I come up," said Keloğlan, and as he drank he looked here and there to see what he could see. Suddenly he noticed a door in the side of the well. Curiously he opened it, and in a little room behind the door he found a very beautiful girl sitting and embroidering. On the edge of her embroidery hoop there sat a frog.

"Greetings to you!" said the girl.

89

"Greetings to you!" replied Keloğlan.

"Where do you come from?" asked the girl. "And where are you going?"

Keloğlan told her of the caravan and where it was going. Then the girl said, "I'd like to ask you a question, if you will. Tell me, which of us is the prettier, this frog or I?"

"Whichever one loves is the more beautiful," answered Keloğlan.

The girl smiled. "If you hadn't answered my question that way, you would never have gone to Baghdad with your caravan," she said. "Open that door on your right and see what happened to the others, those who answered another way."

Keloğlan opened the door on his right, and he saw a great heap of heads, heads of all the young men who had failed to give the right answer for the girl's question. Quietly he closed the door again.

90   Once more she spoke. "I'm going to give you three pomegranates. In return, you must promise that you will pretend never to have seen me. Just forget about me. When you go home and are with

your wife, cut these pomegranates open. But, remember, you have never seen me!"

As soon as Keloğlan had left the room, he called to the merchants, "Let down the rope. I'm coming up." They let down the rope, and after he had put the pomegranates inside his shirt, he tied the rope around his waist and they pulled him up.

Now Keloğlan had three pomegranates, besides the beltful of gold, which the merchants had let him keep for his great service to them. He put these things into a bag and gave them to a trustworthy man on his way home from Baghdad. "Please give this package to my wife. She will know how to reward you," he said. And the man left with the package. Then Keloğlan continued with the caravan to Baghdad.

One day the innkeeper came to the girl's room. "My sister," he said, "a man just came with this package for you from Keloğlan. Open the door."

She opened the door and examined the package. "Oh!" she exclaimed. "How fine that he has sent all this gold. Perhaps you will take a coin to the man

who brought the package. As for the pomegranates
—well, it seems strange to send pomegranates so
far, doesn't it?" She closed and locked her door, and
then she put the pomegranates on the shelf while
she finished her work.

As she worked, she became thirsty, and at last

she reached for one of the pomegranates. "Keloğlan
was right. Pomegranates were a fine gift," she decided. "And I believe I'll open one right now." She
cut open a pomegranate, but, to her surprise, instead
of hundreds of juicy, bloodred seeds, out came

jewels, all sorts of jewels! Scarcely able to believe her eyes, she cut open the second pomegranate, and it was filled, just filled, with gold. As for the third pomegranate—as soon as the girl had cut it open, out stepped a rooster. "Gahk!" it said, and as it crowed, from its beak tumbled a gold coin. And "Gahk!" it crowed, and there came another gold coin. The girl could barely believe her eyes as she looked about at the things Keloğlan had sent to her.

In the morning, she called the innkeeper. "You are as close to me as a brother, and you must know what I plan to do." Quickly she told him about the contents of the pomegranates, and then she said, "This is what I would like to have you do. Come with me to the market, and let us exchange all these jewels for money. Then I can know better how to manage what Keloğlan has sent."

"All right," said the innkeeper, and they started out. When they had sold all the jewels, they had so much money that they had to carry it back to the inn in huge flour sacks. And still she had the gold and the rooster!

93

"Now, if you will help me, this is what I'd like to do. I want to find a fine house, as beautiful as the padishah's palace, and furnish it with fine rugs and divans, and hire servants to care for it. I want Keloğlan, when he returns, to find a home as grand as a palace."

Day by day the innkeeper helped her, until finally she was able to move into a house even more elegantly furnished than her father's palace. There she settled herself, awaiting Keloğlan's return.

Meanwhile, the caravan was on the way back from Baghdad. When they were one day's distance from the city, the girl heard about it and called her most trusted servant. "Go here and there to all the shops until you have gathered together a full set of beautiful clothes, complete with headdress and fur, to fit my husband Keloğlan. Then go to the south gate of the city, where you will see a caravan coming. Ask for the head porter, my Keloğlan. Take him aside and have him exchange his old clothes for the new ones, and bring him here to me."

Carrying the fine, new clothes, the servant went

the next day to meet the caravan. Sure enough, there it came, *tungur tingur,* with its bells ringing. And in front walked Keloğlan, with his long beard down to his waist, and his boots up to his knees, and his sleeves rolled up. He looked a picture of might!

"Greetings to you!" said the servant.

"Greetings to you," Keloğlan answered.

"I'm looking for the head porter, Keloğlan. Do you know him?"

"I am the one," replied Keloğlan.

Taking Keloğlan aside for a moment, the servant whispered, "Your wife has sent me with these clothes for you. Please be so good as to take off the ones you are wearing and put these on, instead. Then I will take you to her."

Wondering very much at this strange request, Keloğlan busied himself as the servant had indicated, and he looked splendid, indeed, when he had finished. "Aha!" he finally decided. "All this wealth must have come from my wife's father. I am glad he and my wife have been reconciled." At the servant's suggestion, Keloğlan climbed into the waiting carriage, and they

95

went to his wife's new home.

When they arrived there, the door opened and all the other servants greeted them with respect. Bewildered, Keloğlan was led through the fine halls to a beautiful room where his wife awaited him. "What's this? What has happened?" Keloğlan asked.

With a smile and a little shake of her head, his wife whispered, "Later! Later I'll tell you, when the servants have left us." She clapped her hands and called a barber to give her husband a shave. Then she ordered the bath to be made ready, and Keloğlan went in and bathed. When food was brought in, on huge trays, they ate until they were satisfied. And still Keloğlan puzzled and wondered at the remarkable change that had come about in his affairs.

Finally the servants were dismissed, and Keloğlan and his wife were at last free to talk. "I must know!" he said. "Tell me! Where did all this wealth come from?"

"Surely you must know!" she answered. "Well, you remember that you sent me three pomegranates. The first one was packed with jewels, the second was packed with gold, and the third—inside the third was a rooster. And each time the rooster crows, a gold piece drops from his beak. He's in the cupboard. Come and see!"

At last Keloğlan understood the wonderful things that had happened, and he felt very, very happy. "You know, wife," he said, "let's do something to share our good fortune with others. Let's call a crier and have him go all through the town to invite everyone to come to dinner with us. Let us have this kind of feast for three days. And we shall give a piece of gold to each guest for the rent of his teeth."

His wife agreed at once, and the next day they had the crier go out to all parts of the town and announce the feast. Immediately the cooks set to work preparing a banquet—meat and rice and macaroni and vegetables and fruits and delicacies of all kinds just poured into the house and were made ready for the guests. As soon as the food was ready, the guests were served. They ate and ate, until they could eat no more. And as they left, Keloğlan, who sat by the door in his handsome new clothes, gave a piece of gold to each guest who had honored their house by coming and eating.

Now, when the padishah heard about this house where food was served and people were given money, he called one of his servants. "Who is this man who is entertaining the whole town? Is it possible that he may be greater than I am? Let's go there tomorrow and eat there like anybody else. I'll go in disguise, so no one will know me. We'll just find out about this!"

On the second day of the feasting, therefore, the padishah wore the clothing of a merchant and he and his servant went, just like anybody else, to Keloğlan's house. As they entered the house, the daughter saw them and she recognized her father, despite his disguise. "Look!" she said to her husband. "My father is coming with a servant, and they are going to eat here. Be sure to give my father two pieces of gold—two for my father and one for the servant."

The padishah was served with everyone else. He and his servant were offered food, and when they had had coffee and were ready to leave, Keloğlan handed two pieces of gold to the padishah and one to his servant. After they had left Keloğlan's house, the padishah said, "Why do you suppose they gave me two pieces of gold when they gave you only one?" But for this question, the servant had no more notion of an answer than did his master.

Since the feasting was to continue for another day, the padishah and his servant decided to go back again to Keloğlan's house, and at the specified time the next day, they joined the other guests. As soon as the padishah's daughter saw her father enter, she whispered to her husband, "Please ask my father not to leave after the meal, but to stay behind until the others have gone."

When the padishah and his servant were ready to leave, therefore, Keloğlan said to the padishah, "Please, sir, won't you stay a little longer? We'll take you home in our carriage shortly."

Puzzled but curious, the padishah sent his servant home, and he stayed until the rest of the guests had left. When only Keloğlan and the padishah remained in the banquet hall, Keloğlan's wife entered, dressed in a beautiful gown, with gold all around her throat and with a crown on her head. As she walked into the room, Keloğlan said, "Your Majesty, here is your daughter."

Startled, the padishah replied, "No, she is not my daughter."

"But she is your daughter," Keloğlan insisted.

"No," the padishah repeated. "How could this be my daughter? My daughter is gone, married to a poor man, nothing but a *simit* seller, a Keloğlan! This cannot be my daughter."

"Tell me, sire," Keloğlan continued quietly, "is there any sign by which you would know your daughter if you were to find her?"

"Of course I would know my own daughter!" the padishah retorted impatiently. "At the base of the back of her neck, there is a small mole."

As the padishah finished speaking, his daughter bent before him and lifted her hair from the back of her neck. There, right enough, was the mole.

"Oh, my daughter," cried the padishah, embracing her, "I was mistaken. There is indeed someone greater than I am. God is greater than I am. Now listen to me. I am an old man, no longer well fitted to rule. From this time on, Keloğlan, all I have shall be yours—my crown, my kingdom, all shall be yours. And from today until the end of my life, I shall spend my time washing and praying."

To celebrate the occasion, they arranged a wedding that lasted for forty days and forty nights, all anew, fit for a padishah and his wife, and they lived happily together all the rest of their lives. They had their wish fulfilled; may God grant us ours!

Adapted from a story told by Saliha Arel, Sivas, and translated by Neriman Hizir, Ankara, Turkey.

Keloğlan

and the Lucky Exchanges

*O*nce There Was and twice there wasn't, when genies played polo in the old Turkish bath, and when I was rocking my mother's cradle *tungur mungur*—well, in those times there was a Keloğlan who was so strong-willed and stubborn that, once he had his mind on something, nothing could change it. This Keloğlan lived with his grandmother in a poor little hut at the edge of the village.

Now, one day as Keloğlan was walking home barefooted from his neighbor's house, he got a sharp thorn stuck halfway into the sole of his foot. Grumbling and groaning, the boy limped home to his grandmother. After picking here and there with a needle, the old woman was at last able to remove the thorn. "There!" she exclaimed. "Into the stove with the nasty thing, I say!" and she was about to throw the thorn into the fire.

"Wait, wait! You never can tell when something like that will come in handy," said Keloğlan. "Besides, it's given me so much trouble that I ought to get some use from it." Taking the thorn from his grandmother, the boy put it carefully at the back of the stove.

A week or so later, as the grandmother was sweeping the floor, her sleeve brushed against the back of the stove and the thorn fell into the fire and was burned to ashes. "It's just a thorn," said she to herself, "and, like as not, he's forgotten all about it."

But the very next day Keloğlan came rushing in from somewhere or other. Straight to the stove he went and looked for his thorn. "My thorn, Grandmother! Have you seen it? I've just found a fine use for it."

"What use could you have for something so common as a thorn?" asked the old woman.

"Never mind, Grandmother. I need my thorn now. Have you seen it?"

"Well, yes, my boy. As I was sweeping the floor yesterday, my sleeve brushed against the stove and knocked the thorn into the fire."

Keloğlan stared at his grandmother. "You mean it burned? You mean the stove took my thorn, my own, valuable thorn?"

"It's gone, my boy, and that's all there is to it," she said. "Either forget about it or go out to find another thorn. The fields are full of thorns just like that one."

"Not like that one," the boy insisted. "Very well, Grandmother, since the stove took my thorn and can't give it back, I'll take the stove, instead. It's given me so much trouble that I ought to get some use from it." And he had his mind set on having the stove.

Days and days passed, with the grandmother wanting to keep the stove to cook their meals and Keloğlan demanding that the stove be given to him, until finally the old woman could stand the quarrel no longer. "Take it, then," she shouted, "and be off with it!"

The boy took the stove, and, holding it firmly against his chest, he carried it out the door. After a few steps down the road, he stopped to rest. Then, hoisting the stove onto his back, he walked a little farther. "Oof!" he grunted. "This is heavier than I thought. And whatever will I do with it?" Since he was closer by now to his neighbor's house than to his own, he struggled to the door and set the stove down carefully. "May I leave my stove here for a few days?" he asked, as the neighbor came to the door. *107*

"Of course," answered his neighbor. "Put it over in the corner. There it will be perfectly safe."

"I certainly hope so," the boy said, "because it's

a good stove. Besides, you never can tell when a stove like that will come in handy." And off he went about his business.

For a week or so, the neighbor left Keloğlan's stove in the corner, but in truth it crowded the room so badly that it was a nuisance to everyone. At last, on his wife's insistence, the neighbor hauled the stove out to the stable. There it stood, nuzzled by the donkey and the ox, until one day the ox crashed into it and smashed it to pieces. Hearing the noise, the

neighbor came running out. "Oho! there's the end of the bald boy's stove. It's too bad! But, like as not, he's forgotten about it by this time."

Little did the neighbor know Keloğlan if he thought that. The very next day, Keloğlan came knocking at the door. "Good morning, neighbor," said he. "I've come for my stove. I knew if I kept it long enough, I'd find a good use for it—and indeed I have."

"Your stove? Well, you may have it, but it's not exactly as you left it, my boy." And the neighbor led Keloğlan to the stable. There lay the bits and scraps of what had been his stove.

"What's this!" exclaimed the boy. "I left a fine stove, and now I find pieces here and there."

"Oh, but I didn't do it," said the neighbor hastily. "It was my ox. The poor beast was crowded and must have stumbled over it."

"The ox, eh?" mused Keloğlan. "Very well, my friend, I'll take the ox and see what I can do with it. It's caused me so much trouble that I ought to get some use from it. Besides, you never can tell when an

109

ox like that will come in handy."

"Indeed, you will not take my ox!" shouted the neighbor. But he might as well have saved his shouting, for all the good it did him. Day after day, Keloğlan came by to look at the ox and to insist that it was his, until at last the neighbor could stand the torment no longer. "Well, then, take the ox. And don't you ever bring anything to store with me again."

Off went Keloğlan with the ox, but the more he looked at it, the less he knew what to do with it. As he was thinking this way and that about the matter, he heard some music, and, following the sound, he came upon a fine wedding celebration. Now, how was he to go to the wedding feast with an ox? Seeing an olive tree in a corner of the courtyard belonging to the bride's father, he tied the ox securely to a low branch of the tree. Then he went inside to join the guests.

110   For days, the wedding celebration continued, and Keloğlan stayed for all of it. But many mouths eat much food, and at last the bride's father found himself entirely without meat. Slipping out into the

courtyard, he was hurrying to market when suddenly he noticed Keloğlan's ox tied to the olive tree. "How fine!" he rejoiced. "One of the guests has brought that ox as a wedding gift! It couldn't have come at a better time." Speedily he slaughtered it, and in due time, it appeared in kabobs and all sorts of delicious dishes.

When the wedding festivities had finally ended, the guests departed, with Keloğlan among the last to leave. To his surprise, his ox was no longer standing in the courtyard. "My ox! Where is my ox?" he shouted, running here and there as if running would somehow bring the creature back.

Hearing the commotion, the bride's father came over to him. "Your ox? Was that your ox in the courtyard? I wish I had known, my boy. I used it two days ago for the wedding feast, thinking some one of the guests had brought it as a gift for the bride."

111

Keloğlan looked at him, disbelieving. "You killed it? You ate my ox, my fine ox?"

"How was I to know? You shouldn't have

brought it here so that I could mistake it for a gift,"
said the fellow, already quite worn out by the wedding. "Here. I'll give you money for another ox."

But he was not to escape so easily, not when
Keloğlan had made up his mind on the matter.
"There isn't any other ox as good as mine was,"
Keloğlan insisted. "Either give me back my own ox,
or I'll—I'll—I'll take the sister of the bride! That's
what I'll do."

Day after day went by, with the bride's father
offering money for another ox and Keloğlan demand-

ing either his old ox or the bride's beautiful sister, until at last the father could stomach the argument no longer. "All right, you bald boy. Here she is! Take her, and get out of here."

After all, the bride's sister was much more useful to Keloğlan than the ox, so off they went down the road. And for all I know, they are still together.

Adapted from a story told by Hayrettin Kimyon, Antakya, and translated by Ahmet Uysal, Ankara, Turkey.

Keloğlan

in the Service of the Padishah

*O*nce There Was and twice there wasn't, when the flea was a porter and the camel was a barber—well, in those times there was a bald-headed boy, a Keloğlan, who was much more lucky than he was clever.

One night as the boy lay sleeping, he had a dream in which a wise old man said, "Keloğlan, listen to me. As soon as the sun rises tomorrow, you must attach yourself to some wealthy household. In that way, you will find good fortune."

Keloğlan sat bolt upright in bed and looked about him, but there was no one to be seen. "Attach yourself?" he muttered. "Fasten yourself, he must have meant. Well, tomorrow has not yet come," and the boy went back to sleep.

Nonetheless, with the first ray of light in the morning, Keloğlan got up and made himself a bit of breakfast. Then he went out into the street to look for a wealthy household. Up and down and around and around he looked, until at last he came to the palace of the padishah. "Here is a wealthy household. But how am I to attach myself to it?" the boy puzzled. He sat down to think about the matter. Now, quite without noticing, he had sat down upon an open tar bucket, and when he arose, still not sure of what to do, the tar bucket came along with him.

After a considerable struggle, Keloğlan pulled the tar bucket from the back of his baggy trousers. "Now, there is an idea!" he exclaimed. *"Attach—fasten—stick* . . . of course. All I need to do is to stick myself to someone in the padishah's household." And he waited just outside the padishah's gate until the gateman came to open it for the waterman. Quickly Keloğlan slipped through the gate and ran behind the gateman. Backing up to the surprised fellow, Keloğlan stuck himself to the back *117* of the padishah's servant by the tarry seat of his trousers.

"What are you doing?" asked the gateman angrily, as he pulled and pulled, and still couldn't free himself from Keloğlan.

"Oh, you needn't try to unstick me," said the boy. "I was told in a dream to stick myself to a wealthy household and find my fortune there. It's my destiny, and there is nothing you can do about it."

"Get out! Go away!" shouted the gateman, still stuck fast to the bald-headed boy.

Just then, the padishah looked out of his window. "What is all this noise?" he asked.

"Oh, sire, this foolish Keloğlan has somehow tied

himself to me, and he won't let me go," answered the gateman. And he danced about in an effort to loose himself from Keloğlan.

The more the padishah watched, the more he laughed at the silly pair. "Come up, you two, and let me see what can be done for you." Together, the gateman and Keloğlan stumbled along to see the padishah.

It was the matter of but a moment to cut the seats out of both pairs of trousers. Then, dismissing the gateman, the padishah turned to Keloğlan. "Well, my bald-headed boy, what is your name?"

"My father named me Hasan, but I am known as Keloğlan."

"Well, then, Keloğlan, why have you come?"

As Keloğlan explained his dream, the padishah smiled more and more broadly. This funny fellow might indeed make a good addition to the household. "Can you help the cook in the kitchen?" asked the padishah after Keloğlan had finished speaking.

"Oh, yes. Of course I can," he answered quickly. At once he went to the kitchen, and he looked about him here and there as the cook showed him the things he must do. But, somehow or other, the boy always managed to do exactly the opposite of what he had been told by the cook, and before long, the cook had concluded Keloğlan was worse than no help at all.

One day as the cook was about to go to market, he called, "Come here, boy. This is absolutely the last chance you are going to have with me. See those dirty dishes? Well, while I am gone, I want you to wash those dishes and put them away very neatly without breaking a single one." Keloğlan nodded, and the cook went out.

"I'm not to break a single one," Keloğlan reminded himself. "That must mean that I should break them all." And one by one he broke the dishes, washed the pieces very carefully, and piled them neatly in a great pot on the shelf.

"Have you done exactly as I told you?" the cook asked when he returned from the market.

"Yes, sir, and the dishes are all arranged neatly in that big pot," the boy answered.

Surprised, the cook hurried over to look. "What

have you done?" he shouted, as he found that all the dishes were broken. "Get out! Get out!"

"You said not to break a single one, so I thought you wanted me to break them all," said Keloğlan. "And I did."

"Oh, you fool! Get out, I say. Get out of my kitchen. I won't have you here another moment." The cook shouted so loudly this time that the padishah heard him.

"What's the matter? What's going on down there?" he called.

"Oh!" exclaimed the cook. "That Keloğlan! I have had enough of him. Please take him away from my kitchen."

"All right," said the padishah. "Come with me, my boy. You can be my own personal servant." Keloğlan went upstairs with the padishah to see where he was to work. "First, you may go and get me a glass of water. Use the back stairs, and draw the water from the tap just inside the door."

The boy hurried down the stairs, eager to please his master. He had filled the glass and had run back

121

upstairs when suddenly he came face to face with a big mirror. Now, Keloğlan had never seen a mirror before, and when he saw himself with the glass of water, he thought the padishah had sent someone else on the same errand.

"Hey, you!" he exclaimed. "I'm the padishah's servant. He sent me for the glass of water. You stay out of this!" As Keloğlan doubled up his fist, the other servant did the same thing, so Keloğlan became very angry. "So you want to serve the padishah!" he shouted. "Take this glass to him, too!" And he threw his glass of water at the other servant. Of course, the mirror broke, and Keloğlan stood looking all about him, as puzzled as he could be. "But where is he? Where did he go?" he asked as the padishah came out of his room. "I was bringing you the glass of water. Why did you send him, too?"

As soon as the padishah understood what had happened, he said, "You saw yourself in the mirror. It was no other servant, but you—Keloğlan. Haven't you ever seen a mirror before?"

Well, Keloğlan hadn't, and the padishah took

him to another mirror so he could see himself in it. "Hmm," said the boy. "Now I know. I'll never make that mistake again."

"Come, my boy," said his master. "I want to sleep for a while. See to it that nobody makes any noise. I don't want to be disturbed at all." And he lay down to rest.

As Keloğlan sat there, everybody was quiet. There was no noise from the kitchen, no noise from the garden, no noise from the street. But there was something going tick-tock-tick-tock. The boy looked here and there, until finally he noticed a strange box on the wall. He tiptoed over, and—sure enough— it was that box making the noise. "Be quiet!" whispered Keloğlan. "You heard the padishah say he wanted to sleep. Stop that noise." But the box went right on tick-tocking. The more it ticked, the angrier Keloğlan became, until finally he tore the box from the wall and smashed it on the floor.

123

"What's that! What's the matter?" cried the padishah, jumping up from a sound sleep to find pieces of his clock scattered all over the floor.

"You told me to keep everything quiet while you slept," explained the boy. "And I told that box to stop making noise, but it wouldn't listen. I gave it just what it deserved!"

"Keloğlan, Keloğlan!" said his master. "Haven't you ever seen a clock, either? You must know that a clock can't do its work without ticking. If it stopped ticking, it couldn't tell me the right time. I meant to have you keep the people quiet, not the clocks!"

"Oh, now I understand," agreed Keloğlan. "I won't make that mistake again." And he sat quietly while the padishah went back to sleep.

A few days later, an ambassador came to the padishah from a king in another country. "Oh, padishah," he began, "the king of my country plans to wage war against your country. There is only one way in which you can prevent this war. Choose an ambassador to represent you. I shall sit on the top of one minaret, and your ambassador must sit on the top of another minaret some distance away. I shall ask your ambassador three questions, forming the questions by signs with my hands. Your ambassador must answer with signs, also. If he answers all three questions correctly, then my king will not wage war against your country."

"How can this be?" asked the padishah. "Let me think about the matter before I agree to it." While the ambassador waited in another room, the padishah thought this way and that, trying to decide on an ambassador able to save his kingdom from war. "If I choose someone who is clever, he'll say the whole business is too ridiculous for him to consider. If I choose someone who is stupid, he's likely not to be able to answer the questions at all. Oh, what should I do?"

Just then, Keloğlan passed the door on some errand or another. Aha!" murmured the padishah. "At least, Keloğlan would have some ideas about it." And he called Keloğlan to him and explained what was to be done.

"Nothing could be easier," said the boy. "I'll do it." And immediately the two ambassadors were taken to separate minarets and each was told to seat himself at the very top of the minaret. As his first question, the foreign ambassador held up one finger. Immediately, Keloğlan answered by holding up two fingers. Satisfied, the foreign ambassador formed his second question by curving his arms out before him to make a flat circle. At once, Keloğlan responded by bending his left arm at the elbow and putting his right hand under his left elbow to show one-half of his left arm. Nodding, the ambassador asked his third question by holding his right hand out with the fingers and thumb hanging down. Promptly Keloğlan answered by holding his right hand out with the fingers and thumb pointing up. "That's all!" called the foreign ambassador, and they both climbed down from their minarets.

"I am happy that my ambassador answered the questions to your satisfaction," said the padishah. "Now would you please tell me what the questions were, and how Keloğlan answered them?"

"Of course," replied the ambassador. "First I said, 'There is one God, is there not?' And Keloğlan answered, 'But you forget that with the Prophet we give reverence to two.' Then I asked, 'The world is round, is it not?' Keloğlan responded, 'Yes, but you must remember that half of it is land and the other half is water.' Finally I asked, 'Rain comes down from above, does it not?' And Keloğlan answered, 'True, but plants grow from the bottom up.' You have a very clever ambassador, sire. Since he has answered all of my questions correctly, there will be no war between our countries." And the foreign ambassador left the palace to carry the message to his king.

"This is most interesting," the padishah murmured. "I am curious to hear Keloğlan's report of the conversation." And he called the boy to him. "Tell me," he said, "exactly what questions were asked, and exactly how you answered them."

"Yes, sir. First he asked, 'I am cleverer than you, am I not?' And I answered, 'It would take two of you to be as clever as I am.' Then he asked, 'Do you see how big a tray of pilav I can eat?' I answered, 'That is just half as much as I can eat!' Finally, he asked, 'Do you know that we have five armies ready to send down upon your country?' And, of course, I answered, 'Yes, and my padishah has five generals, each with a sharp sword, to meet those armies and destroy them!' "

"Well done, my boy! No one in my kingdom could have answered more wisely than you have done," smiled the padishah. "You have saved the kingdom from war, and from now on you can be sure of work in my palace. All your life you will be a part of my household."

Keloğlan nodded. "You see, sire? That old man in my dream was right! I attached myself to some wealthy household, and I have indeed found good fortune."

Three apples fell from the sky. One was for the teller of this story, another for the hearer of this story, and the third for the child who might one day read it in a book.

Adapted from a story told by fifth-grade students at Ayse Abla Ilkokulu. Translated by Dikmen Gürün, Istanbul, and in part, by Neriman Hizir, Ankara, Turkey.